miss seeing a single dog! In the first few
kennels were a huge slobbery boxer with
dark eyes and a broad doggy grin, a big
Labrador playing with a chew toy, and a
jumpy, wiry little dog. Izzy didn't know what
breed he was but he looked like lots of fun.
Woof, woof! he barked as she looked in, as if
to say, "Have you come to play?"

Izzy shook her head sadly. She wished
that she could take them all home, but it
was good that there was a place like
Battersea where they could all stay until they
found their families. "Your new owner will
come soon, I promise," she whispered to the
little dog.

"Come on, Izzy!" Aunt Katherine called.
Izzy ran the rest of the way down the corridor.
Auntie Katherine and Uncle Howard were
smiling down at the pen in front of them.
Izzy peered through the mesh . . . and stared
into a pair of beautiful twinkly black eyes.

Battersea Dogs & Cats Home series?

JESSIE'S
story

by

Sarah Hawkins

Illustrated by Sharon Rentta
Puzzle illustrations by Jason Chapman

RED FOX

BATTERSEA DOGS AND CATS HOME: JESSIE'S STORY
A RED FOX BOOK 978 1 849 41583 5

First published in Great Britain by Red Fox,
an imprint of Random House Children's Publishers UK
A Random House Group Company

This edition published 2012

1 3 5 7 9 10 8 6 4 2

The Random House Group Limited supports the Forest Stewardship Council
(FSC®), the leading international forest certification organization. Our books
carrying the FSC label are printed on FSC®-certified paper. FSC is the only
forest certification scheme endorsed by the leading environmental
organizations, including Greenpeace. Our paper procurement policy can be
found at www.randomhouse.co.uk/environment.

MIX
Paper from
responsible sources
FSC   FSC® C016897
www.fsc.org

Set in 13/20 Stone Informal

RANDOM HOUSE CHILDREN'S PUBLISHERS UK,
61–63 Uxbridge Road, London W5 5SA

www.kidsatrandomhouse.co.uk
www.totallyrandombooks.co.uk
www.randomhouse.co.uk

Addresses for companies within The Random House Group Limited
can be found at: www.randomhouse.co.uk/offices.htm

THE RANDOM HOUSE GROUP Limited Reg. No. 954009

A CIP catalogue record for this book is available from the British Library.

Printed and bound in Great Britain by
CPI Bookmarque, Croydon, CR0 4TD

Turn to page 91 for lots
of information on
Battersea Dogs & Cats Home,
plus some cool activities!

❖ ❖ ❖ ❖

Meet the stars of the Battersea Dogs & Cats Home series to date . . .

Bailey

Chester

Misty

Max

Rusty

Daisy

Snowy

Huey

Stella

Angel

Alfie

Cosmo

Coco

Buddy and Holly

Petal

Suzy

Bertie

Jessie

Summer Surprise

Izzy looked at her suitcase and sighed. Last time she'd used it, she'd had to sit on it while Mum closed the zip because it was so full of her favourite clothes, her swimming goggles and even a bucket and spade. But she wasn't going on an exciting holiday this time. She looked round her room sadly. If it had taken so long to pack a suitcase, how long would it take to pack everything she owned?

Izzy sat on her suitcase and rested her head on her knees. She didn't want to go. She didn't want to move house, and she didn't want to stay on Aunt Katherine and Uncle Howard's farm for a month while Mum and Dad got everything settled. And she especially, definitely, didn't want to be in the countryside where there was nothing to do. All her friends would be spending the summer having loads of fun together and she'd be stuck in a field talking to cows and sheep.

"Well, that's not a happy face," Mum said from the doorway.

Izzy turned round and flopped on the bed, burying her face in the pillow. "That's because I'm not happy," she said, her voice muffled. "If you wanted me to be happy you wouldn't be sending me away all summer."

Mum sat down on the bed and pulled Izzy over so her head was resting in her lap. Then she peered down at her, her brown eyes kind, and smoothed Izzy's blonde fringe away from her forehead. Izzy felt herself snuggling into her hug.

"Honey, it's going to be no fun at the new flat." Mum sighed. "There will be boxes everywhere and dust and dirt. Daddy and I need to do lots of work on it to make it nice, and we won't be able to look after you at the same time."

Izzy pulled away again. "I don't need looking after," she pouted at the wall. "I can help you, or I can go to my friends' houses."

"But we'll be too busy to take you over to your friends all the time." Mum sighed again. "I'm going to miss you very much, love, but honestly, it's better this way. Daddy and I can get everything ready so it's lovely for when you come home, and you'll have a great time out in the fresh Yorkshire air with Auntie Katherine and Uncle Howard." She stroked Izzy's back. "You loved the farm last time you stayed there . . ."

Izzy stayed facing the wall. "I was five. I can't even remember it. And you were there." She pouted. "This is going to be the worst summer ever."

Mum started to say something else, but she was interrupted by the cheerful *beep-beep* of a car horn outside. Izzy felt the bed shift as Mum stood up to look out of the window. Curious, she turned over to see who it was.

"It's Auntie Katherine and Uncle Howard!" Mum announced.

Izzy felt panicky. They weren't supposed to be coming until next week. Had they come to pick her up early? "What are they doing here?" she asked.

"I don't know," Mum shrugged. "Let's go and find out."

Mum rushed downstairs and flung open the door, giving Katherine a big hug. Izzy stayed on the stairs and peeked through the banisters.

"What are you guys doing in London?" Mum cried.

Aunt Katherine waved to Izzy. Izzy gave a tiny wave back. "Well," Katherine smiled. "We've come down to London on a special mission, and we wondered if Izzy would help us with it."

Mum turned to Izzy and gave her a look that meant *be polite*. Izzy stood up and made herself smile. "OK," she said quietly. *It was probably something boring like going to visit a museum. A museum all about tractors*, she thought glumly, *or something to do with fields.*

"We're going to Battersea Dogs & Cats Home to pick out a new dog, and we wondered if you would like to come and help us choose?" Katherine grinned.

Izzy gasped. *They wanted her to help pick a puppy?*

Mum gave Izzy a big grin. "What do you think, Izzy?"

"Yes please!" Izzy breathed. Maybe this summer wouldn't be so bad after all!

Battersea Dogs & Cats Home

Izzy grinned as she got in the back of the muddy Land Rover. She'd always wanted a dog, but Mum and Dad said it wouldn't be fair to keep one in their flat.

"Don't go getting any ideas," Mum said as she kissed Izzy goodbye. "Our new flat will be bigger, but we still don't have a garden for a dog to run around in."

"I *know*," Izzy replied, "but I'm going to be able to play with it for a whole month, so it'll be like he's mine for the summer. If I can't have a puppy of my own, then this is the next best thing!"

"Aye, well there'll be plenty of animals for you to play with on the farm," Uncle Howard said as they pulled away from the kerb. "Most farmers have a pet dog that they take around with them. Sometimes they're working dogs that help out with the animals, but sometimes it's just a bit of company."

"You're so lucky!" Izzy breathed. She couldn't imagine taking a dog with her wherever she went. Even if she was allowed a dog, she definitely wouldn't be allowed to take him to school!

"My collie, Donald, got too old to be running around with me all day, so he's retired now," Howard continued. "He's earned a nice life sleeping by the fire, but I've missed having a pup trotting round my heels.

We've got another pet dog, Beans, but
she's scared of cows, so she mainly stays
in the farmhouse."

"You're going to have three dogs?" Izzy
asked in surprise.

"And four cats!" Auntie Katherine told
her. "But one animal
more doesn't really
matter when
you've got a
whole farm full
of them to look
after."

"We thought
we'd get one
from Battersea
Dogs & Cats Home
this time," Howard told
her. "They take care of all kinds of
dogs and cats and find them nice places

to live and families of their own."

"But don't you need a special farm dog?" Izzy asked.

"Not necessarily," Katherine told her. "Just a friendly one. One that likes animals and doesn't mind getting a bit muddy!"

"Here we go," Uncle Howard said, as the car indicator started to click. "We're here!"

Izzy looked up at the blue sign, a circle with a dog and a cat curled up together. She couldn't believe Battersea Dogs & Cats Home was so close to her flat and she'd never been there. "You'd never think this is where hundreds of dogs and cats live," she gasped, looking up at the building. "It looks like a posh hotel!"

"It is – for cats and dogs!" Katherine laughed.

"We need to find the reception,"
Howard said as he parked the car nearby.
As they went in, Izzy listened as hard as
she could for the sound of barking. But
the reception area was quiet and
peaceful. While they waited, Auntie
Katherine and Izzy looked around the
little shop where they sold tea towels and
calendars with pictures of
animals on, as well
as things for
dogs like
chew toys
and
drinking
bowls.

"Mr and Mrs Pickering?" a lady smiled as she came out of a big blue door at the back of reception. As the door swung shut behind her, Izzy heard the faint sound of barking. Her heart jumped. She couldn't wait to see the puppies!

"I'm Nadine," the lady introduced herself, shaking Katherine and Howard's hands. She led them into a little interview room and started to ask them questions about where they lived and what kind of

dog they were looking for. "A farm, wow,"
she smiled. "A lot of our dogs would love
to have space in the countryside to run
round in, although
we'll need to
make sure it's
one that gets
on with other
animals."

"We were
thinking
that a Collie
or a Labrador
would be
good," Katherine
explained. "And we'd
like a puppy if possible."

Nadine grinned. "Actually, I think I've
got a puppy that would be perfect for
you. We don't often have this breed in,

but someone bought her mum without
realizing she was pregnant, and they
couldn't keep the puppies. We've found
good homes for all her brothers and
sisters, but we've still got Jessie
left. She's an Old English
sheepdog!"

Howard laughed.
"Well, that sounds just
perfect. We've got a
whole flock of sheep on
the farm!"

Aunt Katherine started
asking questions about
Old English sheepdogs,
and how to look after
them. Nadine
answered as she
took them through
the blue door and led

them down a long corridor with kennels
on either side. Izzy let the grown-ups go
ahead as she went from kennel to kennel.
She didn't want to miss seeing a single
dog! In the first few kennels were a huge
slobbery boxer with dark eyes and a

broad doggy grin, a big Labrador playing
with a chew toy, and a jumpy, wiry little
dog. Izzy didn't know what breed he was
but he looked like lots of fun. *Woof, woof!*
he barked as she looked in, as if to say,
"Have you come to play?"

Izzy shook her head sadly. She wished that she could take them all home, but it was good that there was a place like Battersea where they could all stay until they found their families. "Your new owner will come soon, I promise," she whispered to the little dog.

"Come on, Izzy!" Aunt Katherine called. Izzy ran the rest of the way down the corridor. Auntie Katherine and Uncle Howard were smiling down at the pen in front of them. Izzy peered through the mesh . . . and stared into a pair of beautiful twinkly black eyes.

Jessie the Sheepdog

Izzy crouched down and grinned as she looked at the tiny pup. Jessie was fluffy and white with black patches, and both of her floppy ears were black. Her eyes were bright and sparkly, and her stubby tail wagged hesitantly as she stood up.

"She's a bit shy with new people," Nadine explained, "but she's such a cutie when you get to know her."

Izzy had heard of sheepdogs before, like the dog on the Dulux paint advert, but she didn't think she'd ever seen one in real life. Jessie was much tinier than she'd expected, and her fur was short and almost curly. "I thought sheepdogs had floppy hair over their eyes?" she asked.

"They do," Nadine explained, "but not when they're puppies. Jessie's coat will get a lot longer when she's older. For now, she's just an adorable fluffball!"

While the adults chatted, Izzy couldn't take her eyes off Jessie. She was sitting quietly, in front of the door to her kennel, with her head on one side as if she was listening to the conversation too!

"With a bit of training," Howard was saying, "she could make a great working farm dog. They're not called sheepdogs for nothing!"

Woof! Jessie agreed.

"Let's take her down to one of the paddocks and let her have a run around," Nadine suggested. "You can throw a ball for her to play with if you like." She smiled at Izzy. Nadine opened Jessie's kennel, and the little pup looked up at the open doorway shyly.

"Come on, Jessie,"
Izzy called, patting
her legs. Jessie
sniffed at the
doorway, then
slowly walked
towards her. She
waited patiently
while Nadine
clipped her lead on
before she padded over to
Izzy, her mouth open in a doggy grin.

"Hello, pup," Uncle Howard bent down
to stroke Jessie and she
wriggled happily, her
stumpy tail
wagging. Then she
jumped up and
gave Izzy a good
sniff, standing on

her back legs with her paws resting on
Izzy's legs. Izzy knelt down to give her a
hug, and Jessie barked happily.

"She likes me!" Izzy grinned.

Nadine led Jessie outside and they all
followed. Izzy couldn't stop grinning as
Jessie walked along, occasionally looking
up at her to check everything was OK.
"Good girl!" Izzy told her,
and Jessie's tail wagged
back and forth
even faster.

When they got outside, Jessie dashed
off excitedly, running in wide circles
around the paddock.

"Jessie!" Nadine called, but Howard stopped her.

"Let her stretch her legs for a bit, lass," he grinned. Jessie ran round a few more times, then dashed up to them, barking excitedly. Then they took turns throwing the toy Nadine had brought out for Jessie to fetch. After a while Jessie got bored of the game and flopped on the ground, panting. Izzy stroked her back, and she rolled over for a belly rub.

Howard, Katherine and Nadine were talking about how big Jessie would grow, when she jumped up suddenly, as if she'd had an idea. She took off in a wide circle,

racing past them as fast as her little legs
would carry her. Jessie ran so close
behind Katherine that she had to take a
step forward. Then Jessie doubled back
and jumped up at Uncle Howard's knees,
making him move as well.

As the three adults looked at the pup
in confusion, only
Izzy could see
what Jessie
was doing.
She was
moving
them so that
they were all
on the same
patch of
ground. "She's
herding you!"
Izzy giggled.

"Well, look at that!" said Uncle
Howard.

"I guess that makes us the sheep!"
Katherine smiled.

"So, what do you think?" Nadine
asked when they'd stopped laughing. Izzy
held her breath. She could tell that
Auntie Katherine and Uncle Howard liked
Jessie, but did they love her as much as
she did?

Izzy watched anxiously as Howard and
Katherine looked at each other and
grinned. "I think she's
just about perfect,
don't you,
Kath?"

Auntie Katherine nodded.

Izzy gave Jessie a
delighted hug.
"We're going
to have
so much
fun this
summer!" she
promised.
Jessie nuzzled
into her and
gave a huge
puppy yawn.
"I think it's
time for you to
go back to your
kennel," Izzy smiled. "But we'll
be coming to bring you home *really* soon."

All the way back to Izzy's house, Izzy,
Katherine and Howard talked excitedly

about Jessie. "We'll see you next week,"
Auntie Katherine said as they dropped
Izzy off at her front door. "And then we'll
have a week to get everything ready
before Jessie arrives."

Izzy was buzzing with excitement as
she went into the house. She ran
straight past Mum and dashed up
the stairs. "How did it go?"
Mum asked.

"Can't talk now,"
Izzy yelled. "I've
got to finish
packing!"

Jessie Arrives

Two weeks later, Izzy was walking across the muddy farmyard with two Collie dogs trotting ahead of her. "Here, Beans! Here, Donald!" she called. The dogs trotted over, their tails wagging, and she bent down to pat their heads. She'd been at Auntie Katherine and Uncle Howard's farm for a week now, and she couldn't believe she'd ever thought she'd be bored.

She'd done so much already! Everything
was very different from her flat in
London. There were so many animals
everywhere, in barns, in fields, and even
in the farmhouse. As well as Beans and
Donald the dogs, there were four cats that
lived inside, and even a goose called
Buster who wandered in and out of the
farmhouse like he was a person!

On her first day, Uncle Howard had
got up really early and fed all the
animals before Izzy had even woken up.
The next day Izzy had gone with him to
help bring the cows into the milking
shed. Izzy was surprised how friendly the
cows were and how they knew just what
to do, each going into a different stall,
standing side-by-side, ready to be milked.

Uncle Howard had let
her try some of the
fresh milk. It tasted
much creamier than
milk from the shops.

She'd also been
busy getting things
ready for Jessie. Nadine
from Battersea Dogs &
Cats Home had already
visited the farm, and agreed that it would
be a lovely place for Jessie to live, but she
and Auntie Katherine had decided that it
would be best to only let Jessie go in the
farmhouse and the garden for a little
while until she settled in. If she went out
in the farm straight away she might get
lost, or be scared of the animals. Auntie
Katherine had asked Izzy to make sure
that the large farmhouse garden didn't

have any loose fence panels or holes that
Jessie could escape through. Izzy had
found several big holes that Uncle
Howard had patched up with old wood
and wire.

Every night
when she spoke to
her mum and dad
Izzy had lots of
new and exciting
things to tell them.
But although she'd
loved getting to know
Donald and Beans and

all the farm animals, she couldn't wait
for Jessie to arrive – and she was coming
today! Because she'd helped to pick her, it
felt a bit like Jessie was her puppy too.

"She is mine," she said to Donald and
Beans. "For the summer, anyway."

Suddenly, the cows started mooing, and the dogs leaped to their feet. *Woof!* Donald barked, pottering towards the farmhouse. Seconds later, Izzy heard the sound of Uncle Howard's Land Rover on the gravel of the driveway. "Jessie!" she gasped.

Izzy ran towards the farmhouse as fast as she could, her blonde hair flying out behind her.

Howard was parking the Land Rover, and there, in the back of the car, peering out of the window, was Jessie's little white furry face. Izzy waved excitedly. When Jessie spotted her she started to bark inside the car. Uncle Howard smiled and honked the horn.

"Stay," Izzy said firmly to Donald and Beans, while she went over to the car door. Donald sat down. He whined gently, and his tail brushed the gravel of the drive, but he didn't move.

Uncle Howard scooped the little puppy up in his arms and opened the car door. *Woof! Woof!* Jessie barked happily when she saw Izzy.

Izzy rushed over and Jessie almost
jumped out of Uncle Howard's arms in
her hurry to say hello.

"I thought I heard voices!" Aunt
Katherine came out of the barn and
grinned when she spotted Jessie. Jessie's
tail started wagging so fast that Izzy
could feel it bumping against her arm.

"Let's take her into the garden." Uncle
Howard carried Jessie through the house
and out the back door. Then he slowly
lowered the puppy to the ground, keeping
a firm hold on her lead.

Donald and Beans followed. They had
already been introduced to Jessie at
Battersea Dogs & Cats Home, but they
gently approached her to say hello.

"Good boy, Donald. Good girl, Beans,"
Uncle Howard praised them as they
sniffed the new arrival.

Jessie sniffed them back and her tail
wagged delightedly.

"It looks like she's going to settle in fine,"
Katherine laughed. "Let's give her a chance
to have a wee, then bring her inside."

"Do you want to hold her lead, Izzy?"
Uncle Howard asked. "We'll let her run
around without one once she's settled in,
but this is safer until she knows her way
around."

Izzy nodded. She felt a tingle of
excitement as she walked Jessie into the
farm house. Jessie followed the older dogs
excitedly, pulling at her lead as she
ran from one to the other.

Once they got through the back door, Izzy stopped to pull off her wellies, but Jessie followed Beans and Donald as they rushed inside, pulling sharply on the lead.

"Arrgghh!" Izzy yelled as she toppled over, letting go of the lead. "Jessie!" she called in horror, as the little puppy raced away.

Herding Games

Izzy gasped as Jessie scampered off, the
lead trailing between her tiny legs, but
Auntie Katherine just laughed. "Don't
worry – look!" She grinned. Jessie had
followed the other dogs up to their water
bowl, and pushed in next to them to
have a drink. Izzy giggled as she saw
Jessie's little puppy bum poking out
between their two big ones.

Once he'd had a drink, Donald raced over to one of his toys and sat down with it between his front paws. He stared at Jessie as she rushed over to sniff it. *Woof!* he barked, making Jessie jump back in shock.

"He's worried Jessie's going to take his toys!" Izzy chuckled.

Katherine smiled. "I haven't seen him move so fast in ages! He and Beans are going to love having a new puppy to keep them on their toes."

Once they'd all had a drink, Izzy opened the back door and let the three dogs out into the garden again. Jessie shot outside, then came running back to Donald and Beans, barking excitedly. Izzy looked at Donald's expression and laughed.

"She only wants to play, Donald," she
said, stroking his grey-streaked ears.

But Donald wasn't interested in
running about.
He padded
outside and
flopped down
in a shady
patch. Jessie
buzzed round
him like a fly,
rushing up to jump
at him, then running away before he
could catch her.

Beans stood a little way away,
watching the tiny whirlwind in
amazement. Jessie lay down low on her
belly and looked at the dogs as if she was
working something out. Then she took
off, running in wide circles around Beans,

Donald and a couple of ducks that were sleeping in the grass. The ducks quacked and flapped their wings, and Beans edged closer to Donald. One of the ducks tried to waddle towards the house, but Jessie chased after him until he was back with the others.

"Auntie Katherine, Uncle Howard, come and look what Jessie's doing!" Izzy giggled. By the time they arrived, Jessie had every animal in the garden sitting in one small patch of grass, all crammed in next to Donald, who was looking at the new puppy grumpily.

Jessie was panting happily, when
suddenly Buster the goose waddled out of
the farmhouse. Jessie skidded to a halt
and crouched flat on the grass. "Jessie—"
Izzy tried to warn her, but it was too late.
The tiny pup took off, running straight
towards the goose.

"Watch out, Jessie!" Izzy yelled,
lunging for the little pup, but before she
could grab her, the goose turned around,
rose up to its full height, flapped
its wings and hissed
loudly.

Jessie shot back towards Izzy and
hid behind her. Izzy smiled and stooped

to pick up the naughty dog. "You might love living on the farm already," she laughed, kissing Jessie on the top of her furry head, "but it might take the other animals a little while to get used to you!"

*

Over the next two weeks, Izzy spent every second with Jessie. She was just the most adorable thing ever! The little sheepdog had settled in so well that Uncle Howard and Auntie Katherine had agreed that Izzy could take her out and about on the farm. Jessie was still fascinated by all the other animals, and it made Izzy giggle when the pup tried to play with the goats and the ducks. Jessie had been so

interested in the cows in
the milking shed that
she'd got too close
and one of them
had almost sat
on her!

They were just
walking into the
farmhouse when the phone
rang. "Izzy!" Auntie Katherine yelled. "It's
your mum!"

Izzy ran inside and picked up the
phone. "Hi, Mum," she grinned,
watching as Jessie started stalking Bluey
the cat, crouching low on the
floor and watching as she
washed her paws.

"Oh, honey, it's so good
to talk to you, are you
having fun?" Mum asked.

"Yes!" Izzy started telling her all about what she and Jessie had been up to.

"That sounds brilliant, love." Mum laughed. "We've been busy here too. Daddy and I have finished painting the kitchen, and tomorrow we're going to start on your bedroom. I got some of that blue paint we talked about, to match your duvet, and we've got you a brand new wardrobe, and a desk for you to do all your schoolwork on. Won't that be nice? Is there anything else you'd like?"

Izzy started to feel sad. There was only one thing that she wanted, and she knew she couldn't have her. She just couldn't get excited about her new bedroom.

The sooner it was finished the sooner she wouldn't be seeing Jessie every day. "That all sounds great," she mumbled.

"What's up, Iz? You don't sound very happy . . ." Mum asked.

A meow and a hiss made Izzy look up. Bluey was standing in front of the kitchen door and Jessie was blocking her path, moving backwards and forwards to stop her from leaving. Her short tail wagged frantically, but Bluey's was waving dangerously as she reached out a paw to scratch the pup that was annoying her. Luckily Jessie was too fast and she jumped out of the way. With another hiss, Bluey turned tail

and stalked off, jumping up on the
kitchen table and glaring down at Jessie.

Izzy couldn't help giggling. "Sorry
Mum, I've got to go – Jessie's trying to
herd a cat!" Izzy put the phone down and
sat on the floor. Jessie ran over to her and
jumped in her lap, reaching up to lick
her on the nose. The puppy settled down
in her arms and gave an enormous
yawn. Izzy hugged her close and kissed
the top of her furry head as tears came to
her eyes. She couldn't bear the thought of
going home – she loved
Jessie so much.

"Oh, Jessie,
what am I going
to do without
you?" she sobbed.

Jessie the Sheepdog

The next day Izzy and Jessie were just leaving the farmhouse when there was a *beep-beep* behind them, and Uncle Howard came whizzing past on his quad bike. "Jump in!" he said. On the back of the bike was a trailer with a haystack on it.

"Where?" Izzy asked.

"In the trailer," Uncle Howard

laughed. "If you sit on the haystack
you'll be right comfy."

Izzy wasn't so sure. Uncle Howard
reached behind and helped her up, and
Jessie bounded up next to her.

"All aboard!" Howard grinned. "Hold
on tight, lass."

Izzy put her arm round Jessie and the
dog flopped down on the straw next to
her, panting happily.

"This is the lower field," Howard explained as he drove into a steep grassy paddock. "We moved the sheep down here yesterday to eat the new grass. When you've got sheep you never need a lawnmower," he joked. The sheep scattered as the bike drove past them, and Jessie sat up excitedly, her ears flapping in the wind as the trailer bumped along. Izzy laughed out loud at the pup's excitement. *How could I ever have thought that the countryside would be boring?* she wondered.

And just as she was thinking that, Jessie jumped out of the moving trailer!

"Uncle Howard, STOP!" Izzy yelled.
Howard cut the engine immediately, and
Izzy pointed, her heart thudding, to
where Jessie was tearing around the field.

"She's OK, lass," Uncle Howard
reassured her. "If she'd hurt herself she
wouldn't be running that fast. Look at
her go!"

Jessie was racing towards the sheep,
chasing first one, then another, making
them bleat and run as she swooped
past them.

"Is that what sheepdogs are meant to do?" Izzy asked.

"No," Howard replied, "but most of them go a bit crazy when they see sheep in a field for the first time, and she is very young. She'll have to be at least five months old before I start trying to train her."

Jessie shot past them again, her tongue hanging out in delight. Uncle Howard gave a piercing whistle and yelled "JESSIE, HERE!" in a cross voice.

Jessie stopped, gave one more longing look at the sheep, and then came back towards them, panting heavily. "BAD DOG." Howard said firmly.

Jessie looked up at him with sad eyes and Izzy melted. She couldn't be cross with her, Jessie was just so sweet!

Uncle Howard winked at her. "She has to learn not to worry the sheep too much, and not to jump out of the trailer," he explained. "She was OK this time, but she might have injured herself. It's important to train a dog properly, to make sure they don't do anything to hurt themselves or anyone else – so a good dog owner has to tell their pet off sometimes."

Jessie gave a whine and lay down on the grass. Uncle Howard looked at her sternly, and then his face softened. "Up!" he pointed to the trailer and Jessie jumped in. "Good dog," he smiled, petting her ears. As Izzy sat next to her on the haystack, Jessie's stumpy tail was wagging again.

At the top of the field, Howard stopped to open a gate, then drove them into the upper field. He parked the bike in one corner, then he lifted Izzy out of the trailer. He went to pick Jessie up too, but she jumped out on her own, landing neatly at Izzy's feet and wagging her tail happily.

"Good lass," he said, ruffling Jessie's ears.

Uncle Howard strode along a path at the edge of the field, next to a fence. Jessie tore ahead, sniffing everything she passed. Suddenly she stopped and ran over to the fence. Behind it was a thick hedge. She started sniffing frantically, running up and down next to it.

"Oh look, that bit of fence is broken," Izzy noticed. She'd spent so long making the farmhouse garden safe for Jessie she was used to spotting little holes a puppy could escape through.

"Well spotted." Howard kneeled down and moved the wire in front of the hole. Jessie sniffed around the wire and gave a small whine.

"Come on, Jessie," Howard said, tapping his leg. "Here, girl." He and Izzy walked on a bit further, but Jessie stayed by the fence. When Izzy looked back at her she just lay down and stared at the fence.

"Is she OK?" Izzy asked.

"She'll catch us up in a minute," Howard said. "Come on."

But although Jessie whined when they walked further away, she didn't move.

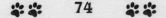

"Maybe there's something there?" Izzy suggested.

"She's probably just smelled a rabbit or something," Howard said, but he sounded less sure than before.

After they'd gone a bit further and the puppy still hadn't come bounding up to them, Izzy was feeling really worried. They couldn't leave Jessie all on her own,

she was only a baby. Uncle Howard kept
glancing back too.

When Jessie was just a little white dot
next to the hedge, Izzy couldn't stand it
any more. "Please can we go back?" she
pleaded.

Uncle Howard gave a deep sigh. "OK,
I guess we'd better. She's definitely acting
funny. But if it is just a rabbit, than that

little pup is going to be
in BIG trouble!"

Izzy ran
over to Jessie.
Jessie sat up
and barked
happily
when she
saw them
coming
back, but
she still
didn't move.
Izzy crouched
down and gave
Jessie a hug, and Uncle
Howard started to climb over the fence.

"What has got you so interested then,
Jess?" he muttered. Jessie jumped all over
Izzy excitedly as Howard used his

walking stick to move the twigs aside.

"I don't believe it!" Uncle Howard
exclaimed. "Izzy, look!"

Izzy jumped up to look over the fence.
There, cowering in the bush, was a tiny
lamb!

Lucky the Lamb

As Howard picked up the shivering little lamb and wrapped it in his jacket, Izzy stroked Jessie's head. "Well done, Jessie!" she gasped.

"Well done indeed," Howard added. "This little one must have been out here all night long. If it wasn't for Jessie, I don't think she'd have made it through the night."

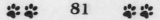

Jessie trotted in front
of them proudly as
they walked
back to the
quad bike.

"Can you
hold the
lamb while
I drive?"
Howard
asked Izzy.

"OK!" Izzy
grinned. She
climbed into the trailer
and settled down on the haystack. Then
Uncle Howard passed her the little
bundle, and Izzy rested it on her lap. The
lamb sat quietly, wrapped in Uncle
Howard's coat. She was still shivering,
and Izzy rubbed her back gently.

"Good dog, Jessie," Howard said,
bending down to ruffle her head. "You
can have a big treat when we get home."
Jessie's stubby tail wagged hard as she
heard the word treat.

Then she leaped up
into the trailer and
scrambled onto
the haystack
next to Izzy. She
sniffed the
lamb, and the
lamb looked up
and gave a
weak *maa*.

"She's saying
thank you!" Izzy
giggled.

"She's a very lucky lamb," Howard
said, starting the engine. "Jessie didn't

lose interest, and she stayed with her
even when we left. It was probably really
hard for her to see us walking away, but
she wouldn't leave the
lamb. Not many
sheepdogs would do
that, let alone an
untrained
puppy."

"So she is
going to be
a great
sheepdog, after
all!" Izzy said
proudly. She
reached out her spare
hand to stroke Jessie's soft fur, and Jessie
panted happily.

"She certainly is." Howard grinned.

*

When they got back to the farmhouse,
Uncle Howard carried the lamb inside,
and put her down in a warm spot next to
the fire. When Donald and Beans came
over to investigate, Jessie stood in front of
her protectively. The lamb was a bit
shaky, and she kept giving tiny, weak
bleats.

Uncle Howard went to get her a bottle.
Izzy watched as Jessie settled down next
to her to keep her warm.

Uncle Howard came back with a warm
bottle with a long dropper at the end. It
looked just like a baby's bottle, but much
bigger. "Now then," he said, putting the
lamb on Izzy's lap. "Hold the bottle and
let's see if she'll drink."

"Me?" Izzy asked. Howard
nodded. Izzy took the
bottle and held it
up to the lamb's
mouth. But the
lamb just turned
her head away.

"Come on,
Lucky," Izzy
pleaded. "Have
some milk."

"Lucky?" Howard raised his eyebrow.

"Well, you said she was lucky Jessie found her," Izzy explained.

"So I did." Howard smiled.

Izzy moved the bottle closer to Lucky's mouth, and this time it went in. "Good girl, Lucky!" Izzy grinned.

Woof! Jessie barked, as the lamb started to suck hungrily.

When the lamb had finished, she fell
sound asleep. Uncle Howard
gently lifted her off of
Izzy's lap and took her
out to the barn to
find her mum. As
soon as the lamb
left Izzy's lap, Jessie
jumped up onto it
and snuggled down,
giving a big puppy yawn.

"You've had an exciting day, haven't
you, Jessie?" Izzy smiled, twirling one of
her soft black ears round her fingers. "But
then every day here is exciting for you,
with lots of room to run around, and lots
and lots of animals to herd!"

Izzy gave the sleepy puppy a big hug,
as she realized how much Jessie loved
being on the farm. She wouldn't enjoy

being stuck in a flat at all. This was where she belonged.

"I'm going to miss you so much when I go home," she whispered, "but I'll think of you running around and playing with poor old Donald. And I'll visit you all I can, and come and stay every summer."

Jessie looked up at Izzy and grinned as if she understood every word. Then she snuggled back down in her lap, and rested her paws on Izzy's arms. Even if they didn't see each other every day, they would always be best friends.

Read on for lots more . . .

🐾🐾🐾🐾

Battersea Dogs & Cats Home

Battersea Dogs & Cats Home is a charity that aims never to turn away a dog or cat in need of our help. We reunite lost dogs and cats with their owners; when we can't do this, we care for them until new homes can be found for them; and we educate the public about responsible pet ownership. Every year the Home takes in around 10,000 dogs and cats. In addition to the site in southwest London, the Home also has two other centres based at Old Windsor, Berkshire, and Brands Hatch, Kent.

The original site in Holloway

History

The Temporary Home for Lost and
Starving Dogs was originally opened in a
stable yard in Holloway in 1860 by Mary
Tealby after she found a starving puppy in
the street. There was no one to look after
him, so she took him home and nursed
him back to health. She was so worried
about the other dogs wandering the streets
that she opened the Temporary Home for
Lost and Starving Dogs. The Home was
established to help to look after them all
and find them new owners.

Sadly Mary Tealby died in 1865, aged
sixty-four, and little more is known about
her, but her good work was continued. In
1871 the Home moved to its present site
in Battersea, and was renamed the Dogs'
Home Battersea.

Some important dates for the Home:

1883 – Battersea start taking in cats.

1914 – 100 sledge dogs are housed at the Hackbridge site, in preparation for Ernest Shackleton's second Antarctic expedition.

1956 – Queen Elizabeth II becomes patron of the Home.

2004 – Red the Lurcher's night-time antics become world famous when he is caught on camera regularly escaping from his kennel and liberating his canine chums for midnight feasts.

2007 – The BBC broadcast *Animal Rescue Live* from the Home for three weeks from mid-July to early August.

Amy Watson has been working at
Battersea Dogs & Cats Home for eight
years and has been the Home's Education
Officer for four years. Amy's role means
that she regularly visits schools around
Battersea's three sites to teach children
how to behave and stay safe around dogs
and cats, and all about responsible dog

and cat ownership. She also regularly features on the Battersea website – www.battersea.org.uk – giving tips and advice on how to train your dog or cat under the "Fun and Learning" section.

On most school visits Amy can take a dog with her, so she is normally accompanied by her beautiful ex-Battersea dog, Hattie. Hattie has been living with Amy for three years and really enjoys meeting new children and helping Amy with her work.

The process for re-homing a dog or a cat

When a lost dog or cat arrives, Battersea's Lost Dogs & Cats Line works hard to try to find the animal's owners. If, after seven days, they have not been able to reunite them, the search for a new home can begin.

The Home works hard to find caring, permanent new homes for all the lost and unwanted dogs and cats.

Dogs and cats have their own characters and so staff at the Home will spend time getting to know every dog and cat. This helps decide the type of home the dog or cat needs.

There are three stages of the re-homing process at Battersea Dogs & Cats Home. Battersea's re-homing team wants to find you the perfect pet: sometimes this can take a while, so please be patient while we search for your new friend!

1 Register details

2 Match

3 Leaving with your new pet

Have a look at our website:
http://www.battersea.org.uk/dogs/ rehoming/index.html for more details!

"Did you know?" questions about dogs and cats

- Puppies do not open their eyes until they are about two weeks old.

- According to *Guinness World Records*, the smallest living dog is a long-haired Chihuahua called Boo Boo from Kentucky, who is 10.16cm tall.

- Dalmatians, with all those cute black spots, are actually born white.

- The greyhound is the fastest dog on earth. It can reach speeds of up to 45 miles per hour.

- The first living creature sent into space was a female dog named Laika.

- Cats spend 15% of their day grooming themselves and a massive 70% of their day sleeping.

- Cats see six times better in the dark than we do.

- A cat's tail helps it to balance when it is on the move – especially when it is jumping.

- The cat, giraffe and camel are the only animals that walk by moving both their left feet, then both their right feet, when walking.

Dos and Don'ts of looking after dogs and cats

Dogs dos and don'ts

DO

- Be gentle and quiet around dogs at all times – treat them how you would like to be treated.
- Have respect for dogs.

DON'T

- Sneak up on a dog – you could scare them.
- Tease a dog – it's not fair.
- Stare at a dog – dogs can find this scary.
- Disturb a dog who is sleeping or eating.

- Assume a dog wants to play
  with you. Just like you,
  sometimes they may want to
  be left alone.
- Approach a dog who is without
  an owner as you won't know if
  the dog is friendly or not.

Cats dos and don'ts

DO
- Be gentle and quiet around
  cats at all times.
- Have respect for cats.
- Let a cat approach you in their
  own time.

DON'T
- Stare at a cat as they can find
  this intimidating.

- Tease a cat – it's not fair.
- Disturb a sleeping or eating cat – they may not want attention or to play.
- Assume a cat will always want to play. Like you, sometimes they want to be left alone.

Some fun pet-themed puzzles!

What to think about before getting a dog!

Here is a list of things that you need to think about before getting a dog. See if you can find them in the word search and while you look, think why they might be so important. Only look for words written in black. They can be written backwards, diagonally, forwards, up and down, so look carefully and GOOD LUCK!

```
I N D E P E N D E N T U N O P M S D H W
S X C V B N H R D G H I L J A N E V X Q
S F T I M E A L O N E M K E R Q U S P
G T H S V V B J P X Z D F E H I Y J T M
A C V B O M G D F D S C T Y A O P R W
F R O U Z C H I L D R E N C Y L I O A K
G D V B I D F J L Q W E V Z L C O Z N R
T G H Y J K L H M N F D S E R T J N G P
M U I L D F G O H K V M F E T Y J K E M
A G H D N C V U B C V P O G M T R I R O
L W X D Z V G S I Z E B F C E X P Z S I
E T Q U A D B E H D L N K Y A E J G L
O R J C C A T T Y P E N B C X S T F H J
R J U J G D X R F H K U F D G Z S G O D
F O R X A O K A Q E N S N M Y I E Q Z L
E N E R G E T I C P A S V F H B N H X K
M W D F B V H N L K G R U O I V A H E B
A S Q E T R Y I D A C X B U K O Y T F C
L Q D S I T R O N G W I L L E D N J M X Z
E H G V N H K G N I N I A R T C I S A B
```

SIZE
MALE OR FEMALE
AGE
COAT TYPE
COST
BEHAVIOUR
BASIC TRAINING
HOUSE TRAINING
TIME ALONE
GOOD WITH: PETS, CHILDREN,
STRANGERS, DOGS
HOW: ENERGETIC, CUDDLY,
STRONG WILLED, INDEPENDENT

Remember: when training a dog,
reward works better than punishment.

Can you think of any other things? Write them in the spaces below.

Tangled Leads and Crazy Maze

Oh dear! The Battersea staff are walking three dogs but the leads are tangled. Can you find out which dog belongs to which person by following the leads?

George

Michelle

Chris

Joe

Spikey

Sammy

Tessa

Start here

Who's walking who?

George is walking _ _ _ _ _ _ _ _ _

Michelle is walking _ _ _ _ _ _ _ _ _

Chris is walking _ _ _ _ _ _ _ _ _

Remember: while in public all dogs must wear a collar and tag and should be kept on a lead.

Remember: always take a poop-scoop bag with you and clean up after your dog.

"Yummy yummy! Three big juicy bones for me," says Tessa, but can you help her find her way through the maze to find the bones?

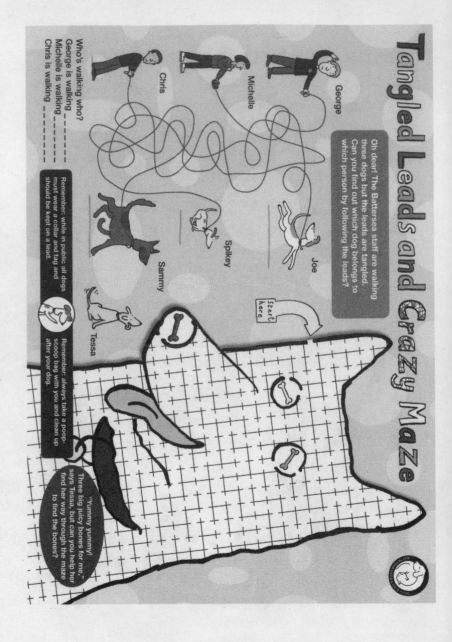

Drawing dogs and cats

If you can draw these shapes you can draw a dog:

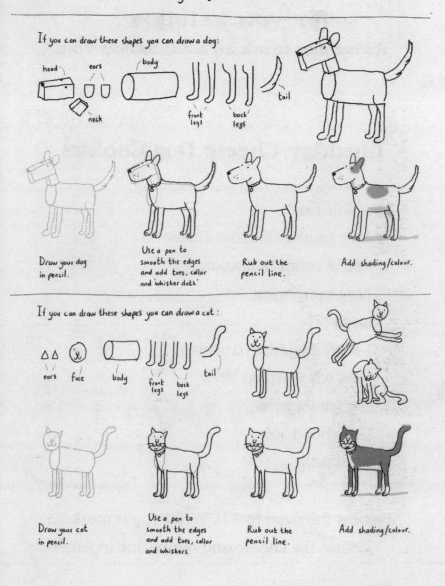

head
ears
body
neck
front legs
back legs
tail

Draw your dog in pencil.

Use a pen to smooth the edges and add toes, collar and 'whisker dots.'

Rub out the pencil line.

Add shading/colour.

If you can draw these shapes you can draw a cat:

ears
face
body
front legs
back legs
tail

Draw your cat in pencil.

Use a pen to smooth the edges and add toes, collar and whiskers.

Rub out the pencil line.

Add shading/colour.

Here is a delicious recipe for you to follow.

Remember to ask an adult to help you.

Cheddar Cheese Dog Cookies

You will need:

227g grated Cheddar cheese

(use at room temperature)

114g margarine

1 egg

1 clove of garlic (crushed)

172g wholewheat flour

30g wheatgerm

1 teaspoon salt

30ml milk

Preheat the oven to 375°F/190°C/gas mark 5.

Cream the cheese and margarine together.

When smooth, add the egg and garlic and mix well. Add the flour, wheatgerm and salt. Mix well until a dough forms. Add the milk and mix again.

Chill the mixture in the fridge for one hour.

Roll the dough onto a floured surface until it is about 4cm thick. Use cookie cutters to cut out shapes.

Bake on an ungreased baking tray for 15–18 minutes.

Cool to room temperature and store in an airtight container in the fridge.

BATTERSEA DOGS & CATS HOME

There are lots of fun things on the website, including an online quiz, e-cards, colouring sheets and recipes for making dog and cat treats.

www.battersea.org.uk